December 20, 1978

The Wobbly Tooth

The Wobbly Tooth

by Nancy Evans Cooney

illustrated by Marylin Hafner

G. P. Putnam's Sons · New York

Text copyright © 1978 by Nancy Evans Cooney
Illustrations copyright © 1978 by Marylin Hafner
All rights reserved. Published simultaneously
in Canada by Longman Canada Limited, Toronto.
Printed in the United States of America
04208

Library of Congress Cataloging in Publication Data
Cooney, Nancy Evans. The wobbly tooth.
SUMMARY: Elizabeth Ann tries very hard to lose a
wobbly tooth.
1. Teeth—Fiction   I. Hafner, Marylin.   II. Title.
PZ7.C7843Wo   [E]   77-14943   ISBN 0-399-20615-9

To Jimmy, Carolyn, Christine, and Mark
—N.E.C.

For Aileen and Margaret
—M.H.

Elizabeth Ann had a wobbly tooth. But this wobbly tooth was different. This tooth was stubborn.

It *wouldn't* come out.

Elizabeth Ann's mother said not
to worry. "That tooth just isn't ready to
come out yet."
But that wobbly tooth bothered

Elizabeth Ann. She decided to get rid of it.

She tried jiggling the tooth with her fingers.

But it wouldn't come out.

She tried brushing with her daddy's
electric toothbrush, with the extra-stiff
bristles, until her arm shook.

But it wouldn't come out.

She tried hopping up and down with
stiff knees.

But it wouldn't come out.

She tried turning cartwheels across the
front lawn until she got dizzy.

But it wouldn't come out.

She even tried munching on her
favorite chewy, nutty, nougat-and-caramel
covered-with-chocolate bar.
But it wouldn't come out.

Elizabeth Ann sat glumly on her
doorstep. She had run out of ideas.

Maybe her mother was right. That tooth
just wasn't ready to come out.

So Elizabeth Ann decided that she
would forget all about that old wobbly
tooth.

She took her best book about wild horses from the corner bookshelf near her bed and started to read. But her tongue kept remembering that wobbly tooth, and kept sneaking over to touch it. She put the book away.

She chewed some bubble gum—only in the left side of her mouth, of course—as she climbed on the old jungle gym in the backyard. But she couldn't blow anything better than a lopsided Ping-Pong-ball-sized bubble. She threw the gum in the garbage can.

She sang her private little "tra-la-la" song as she roller-skated up and down her front sidewalk. The "tras" were just fine, but the "la-la-las" kept bumping into that wobbly tooth.

Elizabeth Ann put her skates back
in the hall closet.

    She sighed.

    She couldn't forget that tooth no matter
how hard she tried!

So when Jane came over to ask her to join in a baseball game, Elizabeth Ann said, "Great!"

She liked playing baseball with her friends. She liked the smell of her leather glove. She liked the lovely *thud* that meant she had made a good catch.

And she especially liked to hit the ball
so hard that it flew over the hedge into the
neighbor's yard.

It was a tough game. First one team
scored, then the other.
Elizabeth Ann was so busy trying to
help her team that she even forgot all
about forgetting.

In the first inning she just missed
tagging a runner out at third base. Later
she hit a fly ball right to the center
fielder.

By the last inning her team was still
behind by one run. Surely she could score
to tie the game!

She stepped up to the plate and
grasped the bat.

The first pitch whizzed by before she
could swing. When the next pitch came,
she was ready.

Crack went the ball when she hit it. It
sailed past first base. So did Elizabeth Ann.

On the ball flew. On ran Elizabeth Ann.
She touched second base and then third.
She headed toward home plate. Elizabeth
Ann saw the ball coming.

She raced faster and faster and finally
slid into home plate in a cloud of dust.

But the ball got there first.
She was out!
Elizabeth Ann sat panting and dusty
and feeling very disappointed. What a
day! Nothing seemed to go right and
now she couldn't even get her run.

She grinned weakly at her teammates.
"I tried," she said.

But Jane cried, "Look!"

Elizabeth Ann looked at everyone else,
but they were looking at her.

"Elizabeth Ann has lost a tooth!"
Elizabeth Ann's tongue flitted over to
feel her tooth. There was nothing but a
hole instead. That wobbly tooth was gone!

She smiled.
It must have been ready to come out
at last.